Ju
F
R24   Reboul, Antoine.
             Thou shalt not kill.

Temple Israel Library
Minneapolis, Minn.

Please sign your full name on the above
card.

Return books promptly to the Library or
Temple Office.

Fines will be charged for overdue books
or for damage or loss of same.

Lost in the Sinai Desert during a battle that separates them from their troops, Slimane, an Egyptian boy, and Simmy, an Israeli girl, stumble across each other in the dark as they try to find their way back to their own lines. Filled with fear and unreasoning hatred they attempt to kill each other.

After a gun duel that lasts all night, Slimane manages to wound Simmy. About to move in to kill her, he is shocked to find she is just a young girl. Stricken with remorse he binds up her wound and helps her recover. Forming an uneasy alliance against the hardships and dangers of the desert, they struggle for survival against thirst, exhaustion, wild animals and burning sand storms. Suspicion turns to acceptance, acceptance to friendship.

A novel of great timeliness, THOU SHALT NOT KILL was awarded the Grand Prize of the Salon de L'Enfance.

Thou Shalt Not Kill

Thou Shalt Not Kill

BY ANTOINE REBOUL

Translated by Stephanie Craig

S. G. PHILLIPS *New York*

Contents

Thou Shalt Not Kill

I

A Boy in Anguish

Dusk shrouded the plateau of El Egma. It was June 10th, 1967, and a shimmering haze rose from the hot sands. In the southwest, the last rays of the setting sun caught the mountain of Moses, turning it a brilliant red. In another hour the shadows would be nibbling away at the outline of the mountain, blanketing the Sinai desert in peace and silence.

Slimane had been waiting for this moment to leave the thorny clump of bushes that protected him from the intense heat of the sun. He was well aware of the risk he faced if he did not use the utmost caution. Walking over the burning dunes in the blazing heat of the day would have led directly to a painful death—lungs and body dried up in the torrid atmosphere.

Slimane was only fourteen, but he knew.

Slimane was afraid. How he longed to escape from this hell! It would have been insane, however, to attempt it earlier, in the burning sun. He wouldn't stir until nighttime. Then he'd pick out the distant mountain and strike out in that direction.

To keep up his courage and to ward off the torpor that comes with intense heat and with not moving for a long time, he went over in his mind the events that had plunged him into this terrible position—alone, and lost in the desert.

✼   ✼   ✼

Orphaned when he was very young, he had been taken in by a peasant of Helouan. At twelve, drawn by Cairo, he had run away from the friendly home of the good peasant and, in Egypt's capital city, had led a life divided between petty thievery and begging.

He had become well acquainted with hungry, joyless days, the indifference of passersby, the rough treatment of the police, and the damp straw of prison cells.

On his release from a spell in prison he had discovered the army. He had noticed that soldiers were more readily moved to pity than the majority of civilians and would quite willingly part with a few coins. And so Slimane fell into the habit of wandering around the barracks at El Gombouria. He explored the area—the college, the Museum of Hygiene, the Abdine Palace, the El Palaki market. But soon the prospect of picking up a little money was no longer the only reason why he turned his steps toward the huge stone structures of El Gombouria.

He had found the regimental kitchens and the windows that opened onto the Rue Bassiouni. He spent many long hours standing there, drawn by the enticing smell of the food being prepared.

One rainy day he sat outside the kitchen, all hunched over, playing up his suffering expression and his miserable appearance until the cooks finally took pity on him. And once the winter came they did more than merely provide him with food. With the kindly cooperation of a lieutenant in the quartermaster corps, they gave him lodging and some decent clothes, asking in return only that he do a few minor chores like peeling potatoes and sweeping the premises.

He had been living in this peaceful atmosphere for two years when the war with Israel broke out.

Slimane remembered Sunday, June 4th.

The regiment, which had been in reserve until then, was assigned to reinforce the road between Nakhl and Akaba. It moved out on the 5th. On the morning of the 6th, as it was installing itself in a defensive position north of El Thamad, it was bombed by enemy planes.

At the first attack, Slimane was ordered to take cover from the murderous assault behind the lines.

That evening, in the silence that followed the noise of battle, he returned to the area of combat. The bodies of a good number of his friends were strewn on the ground beside the guns and tanks and the burnt-out, gutted trucks, many of which were still smoking. Shocked and griefstricken by the disaster to the regiment he had thought invincible, he wondered what to do—how he could help.

The marks of wheels and feet in the sand, heading west, seemed to indicate that the survivors had retreated toward the Suez Canal.

Slimane felt he must rejoin the regiment, not only to save himself but to take part in future battles and avenge his friends.

The 7th, 8th, and 9th of June he had spent trying to reach the track leading from Akaba to Noueiba, in the hope of rejoining the Egyptian forces. The presence of columns of patrolling armored Israeli troops nearby had brought him up short. He could no longer count on finding his friends quickly. He returned to his original point of departure, and it was the evening of the 10th before he came to any decision.

To cross El Egma plateau, one hundred and fifty miles of desert, on foot, was impossible—just as impossible as reaching El Thamad. This was a strategic point, situated as it was on one of the few roads through the Sinai. There was not the slightest doubt that the enemy had already occupied it.

In the end he had chosen the southwest, figuring that he could find the oasis of Bir el Rakaba without running into any serious obstacles. The soldiers, speaking of it in front of him before the battle, had placed it about twenty-five miles from the place where the Israeli planes had bombed them, slightly to the east of a line between that place and Moses Mountain.

Before setting out, Slimane had fortified himself with a goatskin bottle that held nearly fifteen quarts of water and with a knapsack stuffed with five two-pound loaves of bread, a little bag of cornmeal, two packs of cigarettes, and a box of matches, as well as a knife, a rifle, about fifty cartridges, and a military cap.

In an hour and a half, between the weight of the things he was carrying and the sand that gave way beneath his bare feet, his energy was exhausted. He calculated that he had covered about three miles.

That meant more than twenty left to Bir el Rakaba!

But he was determined to keep on until the very end. The next day he would fight against his fatigue; he would force his legs to obey him. He wouldn't give in to his aching muscles. He would be at Bir el Rakaba on the 14th.

❖ ❖ ❖

The winking lights of the stars dotted the sky. There was a light breeze coming from the east. Slimane opened his coarse canvas jacket to catch the cool air of the night. Sitting there in the darkness, he smiled. Nothing was going to keep him from finding Bir el Rakaba.

With the help of Allah!

This comforting thought put him in a better mood. He thought of his cigarettes. How good it would be to smoke a cigarette in the peace of the night, in the middle of the bewitching silence, before setting off again.

Slimane picked up one of the packs and fingered it a moment, turning it over in his hand. He opened it delicately and inhaled the odor before taking out a cigarette and bringing it to his lips.

He postponed the moment of lighting it, imagining the taste of the fragrant tobacco in his dry mouth. Then he decided. The match flared with a vertical, bluish flame, chasing the nearby shadows. He watched it and loved it because of the life it represented, there in the vast, dead desert. The flame consumed the wooden matchstick, burning down till it practically touched his fingertips.

When he had sated himself with the light, he held the match up to the cigarette.

At that instant the silence of the night was torn by the sharp crack of a gunshot.

II

Strange Encounter

A bullet, whistling past his ear, hit the bushes that had been protecting him, and a severed branch struck him on the forehead. He threw himself behind the crest of a dune and plunged his right hand, still holding the match, into the sand.

It was a few seconds before his eyes, which had been fixed on the bright light of the match, could readjust to the dark. As soon as he was able to distinguish shapes again, Slimane raised his head carefully and scanned the neighboring dunes.

It seemed to him that the shot had come from a crest about a hundred yards to his left, although he could not detect any suspicious movement or sound. Overcoming his panic, he picked up his rifle, opened the breech, and put a cartridge into the chamber. Still trembling, he rested the barrel on a low branch of one of the thorny bushes that concealed him and pointed the rifle in the enemy's direction.

❀   ❀   ❀

At sunrise, Slimane was still lying in wait. For hours there had been nothing at all!

It was possible that the enemy, evidently also alone, had chosen to avoid a direct encounter.

But was it necessarily an enemy?

Why couldn't it be a friend?

If so, and if the person who had attacked him had not already fled, the daylight would make it possible to correct the misunderstanding.

Maybe the other person would make a

move and show himself! Slimane would be able to recognize him by his outfit. He would hail Slimane, who would then come out. The road to rescue would be so much easier if he didn't have to travel alone.

At first the thought of this was comforting, but then it occurred to him that perhaps he should be the one to make the first move. What if this stranger (he still wasn't sure it was a friend) was too hesitant or too frightened to move?

Yes, Slimane decided he owed it to himself to take the first step.

But what if the other one was not a friend?

A shiver of fear ran down his back.

He realized, though, that he had to calm down and think instead of rushing into action. He concentrated on breathing evenly, and forced himself to relax his hands, which had been clenched tightly round the butt of his rifle.

Slimane thought things over. It was certainly very possible that this was an enemy. He decided it would be best not to move a muscle.

Bir el Rakaba? Too bad!

Even if he had to stay where he was for two or three days, so what?

Since his life was at stake, the advantage of surprise over the stranger was well worth any temporary discomfort. There was no doubt in his mind that he could play this game of infinite patience as long as necessary.

He took a drink so that he would not have to move again after the sun came up. He settled into a position in which he could remain perfectly still without getting stiff.

Had this movement betrayed him?

Suddenly, from nowhere, a bullet tore through the water bottle and buried itself in the sand next to him. The flying grains of sand struck him in the face.

He watched, stunned, as precious water ran out with an indifferent gurgle and sank into the sand. Before he could begin to think about reacting, a second bullet struck the ground less than a yard from his feet.

With a single bound Slimane jumped to the other side of the dune.

He could judge the direction and the approximate position of the person shooting from the sound of the report. If it was the same one who had fired the night before, he had maneuvered remarkably well. While Slimane had been waiting passively, his enemy had apparently taken advantage of the darkness to circle round him and surprise him from the rear.

✿　✿　✿

The duel lasted for six hours. Very few bullets were exchanged, but the two opponents played a game of hide-and-seek that carried them far to the south of their original position.

Slimane had taken the initiative as soon

as the first moment of confusion was past. It hadn't taken him long to figure out that his adversary was alone. There could be no question now that it was an adversary. He had more than once caught sight of the fleeting silhouette, and, although each glimpse had been too brief for him to take aim, Slimane had been able to recognize the uniform. There was no doubt; his opponent was an Israeli.

Slimane felt a rush of excitement.

He, who had been sent behind the lines as soon as the action had started, he, too, was now fighting against the enemy! And they had thought he was too young!

His mouth twisted in a proud smile.

Too young!

Wasn't it Slimane who sent that man over there scurrying from dune to dune without any chance to escape? Wasn't it Slimane who, with precisely aimed shots, forced him to retreat steadily along the path he himself had chosen, the path to Bir el Rakaba? Wasn't it Slimane, a fourteen-year-old boy, who made an adult Israeli tremble?

✿   ✿   ✿

In the heat of the action, Slimane forgot the sun.

He did not realize how careless he had been until his sight was dimmed by a haze before his eyes.

He checked his fiery excitement, stopped leaping around, and took cover behind a bush.

His clothing was soaked with sweat. He wiped his forehead with the back of his hand, pushing his cap back on his head, and settled into a more comfortable position.

A bullet whined.

Slimane jumped. His patience was running out. The heat and the exhausting duel had strained his nerves. Obviously his enemy was not interested in halting the combat at this point. Victory had seemed so likely, only a short while before, that his opponent's unexpected resistance thoroughly exasperated Slimane. The best thing would be to finish it up as soon as possible.

He decided to try a stratagem.

With the barrel of his rifle he rustled the shrubs that were masking him. A shot rang out.

He rose to his feet, uttered a cry, and fell back into the shelter of the foliage, as if he had been hit.

But, contrary to what he had expected, the enemy remained invisible. Apparently his opponent had seen through the trick. Slimane was furious.

"Who's there," he called, "an Israeli?"

A voice answered: "Yes."

"Dog!" Slimane spat out.

The reply flashed back: "Dog, son of a dog! Egyptian!"

Slimane ransacked his memory, trying to find some insult that would make his opponent start fighting again. Then, suddenly, he saw him crawl across a cut in the dune. He did not seem to be afraid of the risk he was taking.

Slimane raised his rifle, took aim, and pulled the trigger.

A cry of pain followed the report of the shot. A figure rolled down the sandy slope until it finally came to rest far from its rifle, which had dropped from its hand as it fell to the ground.

Sure, now, of his victory, Slimane gave a long, wild shout of joy. And, certain that he was no longer in danger, he rushed toward his conquered enemy.

III
Hate or Friendship?

About ten steps from the figure stretched out on the sand, Slimane stopped, completely stunned. Her arms were crossed, her face turned toward him with eyes closed.

A kerchief had slipped to her shoulders, uncovering a head of thick black hair.

Was Slimane dreaming, or was it really a woman? No, it was a girl!

Looking her over from where he stood, he could see a widening spot of blood on the left leg of her dungarees. It looked as though the wound might be serious, but not fatal.

What should he do? She was still an Israeli.

Slimane's hatred was reawakened. He

wasn't going to spare one of the enemy. But, in spite of his rage, he wasn't entirely immune to pity. After all, she was a girl, and only thirteen or fourteen years old—his own age.

But she was still the enemy.

He struggled with himself, caught in the middle, trying to decide whether to be merciful or to kill her.

The enemy . . . Yes, he decided finally, it was his duty to kill her.

To ease his conscience, he told himself that by finishing her off he would spare her the horrible agony of a lingering death. He would also be acting in accordance with the rules of war. He would be preserving his dignity as a fighter if he obeyed these rules. He would be serving his country.

He raised his rifle and aimed at her forehead. He saw her eyelids tremble and then open. Two large, blue eyes, sparkling in the sunlight, watched him steadily. Her lips parted in a faint smile.

The rifle fell from his hands before he could stop it.

He stood with his arms at his sides and his bare feet anchored in the sand, transfixed by the open gaze that met his own. Her unaccusing eyes, the gentleness of her smile, became unbearable. He looked down.

A warm, lilting voice drew him out of his confusion.

"Hello."

He heard himself reply, "Hello!"

The girl propped herself up on her arms, then fell back again.

"Come on, come over here," she begged him.

She spoke Egyptian well.

Slimane didn't know what to do.

She insisted: "Help me sit up."

He went over, took her under the arms, and set her upright. She pointed to her leg.

"I don't think it's very serious, but it hurts a lot."

Slimane reached for his knife, opened it,

and cut through the coarse material of her dungarees. There were two bleeding holes, a few inches apart, on the outside of her thigh. A flesh wound.

"It's nothing," he said; "I'll wash it."

The words were hardly out when he realized how thoughtlessly they had been spoken.

Water? The goatskin bottle with a hole torn in it that he had had to abandon!

She read his thoughts.

"My canteen," she said, "up there, behind the dune."

In spite of the hot sun and the burning sand, Slimane dashed off and ran clambering up the slope.

The cool, damp leather felt good on his sweaty hands.

Slimane was thirsty, and he drank greedily. The water ran from his lips and trickled down his chest.

When his thirst was quenched, he poured some over his head.

The cleansing did him good. He suddenly felt as though he were awakening from a dream.

Of course! That was it! Only a dream could have induced him to give any help to this girl.

He, an Egyptian, helping an enemy? an Israeli? Oh, no!

He must have been dazed by the long duel, the sun, his fatigue. But Allah was good and had allowed him to get hold of himself again. He had strayed for a moment from the path of duty, but Allah had shown him the way back.

In his haste he had left his gun behind, but the girl's was right there next to him.

He picked it up—a beautiful rifle!—and stretched out on the sand, resting on his elbows. He aimed at the mass of dark hair.

Slimane the Just was about to go into action. He savored this moment. Day of glory! Pride flamed in his heart.

And then, by all the goblins of the Sinai, she moved!

Irritated, he muttered, "Can't you stay still?"

He readjusted the line of sight, gently. A little to the left. There!

She turned her head.

Again, beyond the bead of the rifle, he could see the blue eyes, the smiling mouth.

There was too much trust in those eyes and on those lips. It would be almost cowardly to destroy them.

Slimane gave the problem some thought.

She was an Israeli, he was an Egyptian, and they were enemies. But she was totally defenseless. Besides, she was a girl, and she was only thirteen or fourteen years old.

Slimane made up his mind.

He lowered the weapon of death and picked up the canteen. As he ran down the dune, he shouted, "I was only joking!"

Slimane had chosen to abandon the path of war for that of friendship.

He washed the wounds gently, using the handkerchief she gave him. The touch of the damp cloth soothed her, and she let him take care of her without saying a word.

But the silence disturbed Slimane. Finally he spoke.

"How old are you?"

"Fourteen."

"What's your name?"

"Simmy."

"I'm Slimane."

The sun was beating down on them. Slimane's face was bathed in sweat. He pointed to the clump of thorny bushes at the top of the dune.

"We'd be better off up there, in the shade."

She nodded in agreement and tried to stand up, but the effort made her cry out with the pain.

Slimane rushed forward as she slumped to the ground.

"Here! Lean on me!"

With his help she managed to get to her feet. She took one step, two, and then her muscles gave way. She started to sink down again. Slimane held her up and encouraged her.

"I can't make it," she said.

Their eyes met. The look of despair on Simmy's face was enough for Slimane.

"Let me," he said.

He picked her up in his arms. By Allah, she felt heavy! And that dune and the clump on top looked so far away! Would he ever be able, carrying Simmy, to make it up to the top?

Slimane clambered up, staggering, sinking to his ankles in the burning, shifting sand. He was exhausted and out of breath by the time he was halfway there. His pace became slower and slower. He could feel his arms loosening their grip.

He gritted his teeth, dug his toes into the moving sand, braced his knees, and managed to cover a few yards more. His vision was growing blurred, and, when he looked up ahead, the top of the dune seemed smaller and farther away than it had seemed before.

What martyrdom! And for whom! For what?

Like a flash, the dreadful thought was back: an Egyptian serving an enemy and wearing himself out in an attempt to save her!

He stopped. His fingers started to let go. Surprised, Simmy looked up at him.

"You are so good," she murmured.

Those few simple words worked like magic.

A wave of generosity swept away all Slimane's bitterness. He straightened up, gathered his newly found strength, and set off again, up and up . . .

Simmy was fourteen, just his age. She was a girl, and she was weak. He was strong. He mustn't let her die.

The bushes were nearer now. At last he was close enough to touch them. He had succeeded!

Slimane could have set Simmy down in the shade at once. But he was so happy, even though his arms and legs were throbbing with pain, that he continued to hold her to him.

He sensed that this gesture somehow freed him forever from his murderous thoughts.

I V

Comrades

The sun was cut in half by the line of the
horizon. Simmy was resting on the tent-
cloth, which Slimane had spread out for her
so that she wouldn't get sand in her wounds.

Until now, between heat and fatigue,
neither of the two had felt much like talking. Before settling down in silence, however, they had taken inventory of their resources: almost three quarts of water and a
box of biscuits—enough to keep them going
for two days.

Slimane's own things—the loaves of
bread, the cornmeal, the cigarettes—were
not far away, perhaps an hour's walk. And
the water bottle, even though it had been
punctured, might still have a little water
left.

He would think about that tomorrow. For the moment, the peaceful hush of twilight made the whole problem of their provisions seem very remote.

An evening breeze sprang up, as it always did at this time, and it was soothing after the heat of the day. Simmy and Slimane could now break their silence. They felt the need to talk.

Slimane was the first. He told her about his childhood, about being orphaned, about his misery, his little joys, the friendships of the soldiers, and the circumstances that had brought him to the Sinai. He ended by telling Simmy everything, hiding nothing about himself or his past.

"And you?" he asked, when he had finished.

Simmy had never known her mother and father; she had been brought up by an older sister.

About the middle of May, alarm had begun to spread through Israel. Troops were mobilized. Like the majority of the young

Israeli women, Simmy's sister had been called to serve her country. She was assigned to the Signal Corps but could not bring herself to leave Simmy at the *kibbutz*, the collective farm in Israel, and so she took her along. The understanding leaders tolerated the presence of the younger girl. They even had a uniform made to fit her.

"They wouldn't take me seriously, though," she said, "even when I showed them that I could use a gun. I was just the mascot of the unit."

And then came war.

Simmy went with the troops. First Akaba; on the night of June 10th, they had set out for Noueiba.

Simmy had made a place for herself in a truck at the very end of the column. It was loaded with packing-cases, but she found a ledge about two feet wide at the back and settled down there.

She had dozed off when suddenly there was great confusion and a hard bump, and she awoke to find herself lying on the ground. She had rolled out of the truck. She shouted as loud as she could, but the truck continued on its route.

As she picked herself up, she stumbled over a rifle and some cartridges that had been dragged down with her as she fell. She also found her canteen, her bag containing one ration of biscuits, and her mess-tin. When she had gathered them all together, she set out to try to catch up with the company.

The night was very dark, and she strayed often from the path, finally losing it altogether. With no direction to follow, she was left to wander across the dunes.

The sight of a light appearing out of nowhere had made her panic.

"That was the flame from your match," Simmy explained. "Then I fired. You know the rest."

Sitting there as dusk was falling, Slimane sensed the gaiety in her quiet, young laughter.

He asked her: "When you fired, were you trying to . . . kill me?"

Simmy looked at him and answered steadily, "Absolutely."

"And . . . this morning?"

"I only wanted to see you give up the fight."

"All the same, you aimed well. You got my water bottle."

"I was aiming as close as I could to frighten you. My panic was gone. Really, it was only a game. I don't think I could actually have killed you any more, Slimane. Even so, I'll admit that—"

Slimane interrupted: "But I wounded you. And when I was going to get your canteen, I—"

Simmy, in turn, interrupted him: "Don't go on, Slimane. I know. I, too . . . I'm horrified at the idea of killing. Even so, I was tempted. I'm an Israeli and you're an Egyptian, and I felt bound to do my duty. When you went off to fetch my canteen, if I had

43

been able to move . . . if your gun hadn't been out of my reach . . . You're so good! Please forgive me!"

Slimane saw the tears forming in her bright blue eyes.

"Don't cry," he murmured, taking her pretty, tapering fingers, obviously not meant for handling a rifle, and holding them in his. "I understand, Simmy."

❅ ❅ ❅

In the deepening twilight, they nibbled on biscuits, and each drank a few swallows of water. Shapes grew blurred in the gathering darkness. Soon everything would be blotted out.

The breeze was growing cooler.

Slimane looked at Simmy.

"We have to be careful to protect you from the dew and the cold, because of your wounds," he said.

Simmy looked doubtful. Obviously she could protect herself against the dew; she was already using the tent-cloth he had given her and could roll herself up in it. But the cold! How much protection could the waterproofed material give her against the biting night air of the desert?

Slimane's movements drew her out of her thoughts. He had knelt down and was digging a wide furrow in the ground with his hands, parallel to her position.

"Is that my grave?" she asked jokingly.

"This is a grave you can live in, Simmy."

When he had finished digging the furrow he filled it with branches broken from the nearby bushes and set them on fire. When the small, dry pieces of wood had made a bed of glowing embers, he covered them quickly with sand.

"I wonder why he's doing that," Simmy said to herself. As if he had guessed what she was thinking, Slimane explained: "I'll help you lie down in this trench. The sand will stay quite warm till morning. This way the night won't be so bad for you."

Too moved to thank him, Simmy let herself be picked up and then set down in the trench, which, to her surprise, was really quite warm. A feeling of well-being and gratitude spread through her. Then she remembered that Slimane himself had nothing. Why wasn't he making another bed in the sand for himself?

"Slimane?"

"Yes, Simmy?"

"Aren't you going to dig a bed like mine for yourself?"

How could he admit to her that the biscuit he had eaten hadn't helped the hunger that was gnawing at his stomach? Or, after all the other things he had done that day to soothe and help the girl in his care, that the work he had just finished had used up the last of his energy? He decided not to say anything—Simmy should rest without worrying.

"My body may only be fourteen years old," he explained, "but it's been hardened. I'm used to everything. I could sleep perfectly soundly in a furnace or on a block of

46

ice. You don't have to worry about me. I
hope the night is easy for you. Good night,
Simmy."

"Good night, Slimane."

❁   ❁   ❁

Simmy fought against sleep.

She waited till she could hear Slimane's
steady breathing before letting her thoughts
wander. She felt the need to think over the
strange situation that had brought them so
close together even though they had been
born enemies.

An Israeli and an Egyptian! Different
religions, different races. All the same, they
had helped each other.

She corrected herself: "No, he helped
me." And she thought, "What have I done
for him? Nothing."

And so, moving slowly and cautiously,
she took the tent-cloth that had been covering her and, without waking Slimane,
laid it over him.

V

The First Alarm

Slimane opened his eyes. It was still night. He could tell from Simmy's regular breathing that she was sleeping soundly.

He was satisfied: his stratagem had worked. He had been careful not to move and give himself away when she had covered him with the tent-cloth.

He thought. . . .

The dry little biscuits wouldn't last them even two days.

Even though they had taken only a few swallows from the canteen, how much water could it have left in it? A quart? A quart and a half? Not enough to quench their thirst during the day to come. Slimane's throat was already dry. What would it be like in the burning sun? And Simmy? She was wounded, and, for all he knew, she might even have a fever!

There could be no hesitation. "If we want to stay alive," he thought, "I'll have to go back to the place where we met."

Five loaves of bread! Cornmeal! The water bottle! True, the bottle had a hole in it; but, if Allah had willed so, it might still hold a good portion of its contents. And his cigarettes were there. Even though he had been foresighted enough to stuff the matches into his jacket pocket, he had left the packs of cigarettes in the knapsack with the rest of the provisions.

But it was now time for action.

Slimane slipped out from under the tent-cloth and silently spread it over his companion again.

Afraid that she might awaken and think that he had left for good, he thought of a way to let her know that he had only gone off for a little while. He took off his jacket and laid it next to her bed, along with the

rifles and ammunition, the canteen, the biscuits, and his knife.

If Simmy did wake up, the sight of his
things should reassure her that he had not
gone very far.

He shivered in the cold. Well, the walk
would warm him. Simmy still hadn't
moved . . .

He strode over the crest of the dune and
headed north.

❊   ❊   ❊

It was not the dawn that woke Simmy,
but the vague sensation of some presence,
of something brushing against her.

Even half asleep, she was aware of the
weight of the tent-cloth. Good Slimane! He
had wanted to show that he was as generous
as she had been.

A bump against her side woke her up a
bit more. How touching! Slimane must be
tucking her in!

Another light touch, barely perceptible,

on her shoulders: he was pulling up the cloth, which she must have displaced in her sleep.

Fully conscious now, Simmy was filled with gratitude to the boy who was watching over her so solicitously. It was good to know that she was so well protected.

Only yesterday he had been an enemy, and now, today, he was such a wonderful friend.

What a strange, ironic twist!

✿   ✿   ✿

Slimane tried to figure out just where he and Simmy had been when they started to fight.

Although their movement had been broken by lulls and by the rounds of fire, Slimane placed the spot at a distance of about two miles.

He had calculated well: after a little

more than an hour at a steady pace across the dunes, he found himself right at the place where he had left his things earlier that day.

He recognized the knapsack first, and even in the darkness he could tell it was intact by its bulky shape. The bread, cornmeal, cigarettes—everything was there.

Fear gripped him as he cautiously approached the goatskin bottle. Kneeling, he found, to his surprise, that he had trouble focusing on the bottle. Something seemed to blur its contours. It looked so small . . . He was afraid to touch it. Timidly, he stretched out his trembling hands, only to draw them back again. He was paralyzed by the fear that his hopes would come to nothing. He made an effort to shake off his fear, to reason with himself.

What did it matter if the evil spirits of the Sinai had emptied the bottle? Slimane had enough resources to reach the combat area. Amid the disorder there lay everything that his comrades had abandoned after the enemy bombardment: food, drink, clothing . . .

How far? Only a few miles, and it was still early, no later than midnight. He knew the thought of Simmy would keep him going in case he did have to make the trip.

And now Slimane felt he could face finding out how much water there was left. Without hurrying, he took hold of the flattened opening of the bottle. His fingers closed round the skin and lifted it, just a little. He could hear the familiar sound of water sloshing around. He picked up the goatskin and held it out at arm's length.

It was heavy! It still held at least four or five quarts, and it wasn't leaking! Simmy's bullet had pierced it high up near the neck. It was nothing serious. Tying the leather strap that was used to close the bottle just below the bullet hole would take care of it.

Allah be praised! Allah, who had willed this miracle, who had chased the evil spirits, and who had allowed Slimane to find his supplies again.

*   *   *

Simmy was still musing.

Why should her meeting with Slimane have been merely by chance? Mightn't it have been brought about by the Hand of Destiny? Wasn't it true that the hatred between them, nurtured in their hearts by their elders, had disappeared as soon as they had gotten to know and appreciate each other?

It was strange, this friendship, following so suddenly the racial hatred, the wish to kill. She would have to think about it some more, talk about it with Slimane . . .

But it was not yet light. Simmy felt that this was not the right time to bring up the topic, and so she said nothing.

She listened contentedly to Slimane, crawling about as he tucked in the tent-cloth, which the night wind had raised.

She was marveling at his thoughtfulness when a violent blow on her shoulder made her start.

Had Slimane tripped over her in the darkness?

And where did that hot breath come from, that hoarse panting against the back of her neck?

Simmy turned over quickly, and the wounded leg wrenched a sharp cry of pain from her. It was answered by an ominous growl that sent a shiver of fright down her spine.

"Slimane!" she screamed.

❋   ❋   ❋

Slimane did not linger after closing the bottle. It had occurred to him more than once that he might stop and quench his thirst, or give in to his hunger and take something to eat. But the thought of Simmy, left alone, spurred him on.

He loaded the goatskin bottle and the knapsack onto his shoulders.

He had decided that he would make only two stops to rest on the way back.

At the first halt, he got his breath back in a minute or two and set off again quickly with a light heart.

After the second stop it was much harder to get up again. He was tired from the long, hot day, and weak with hunger. He resisted the temptation to rest longer, though, and, without quite understanding why, he had the feeling that this refusal to yield somehow made him a better person. He knew how much happier he would feel if he took care of Simmy's needs before satisfying his own.

As he struck out again over the sand, he whistled to keep up his courage.

❖   ❖   ❖

"Slimane!" Simmy called again. Why didn't he answer?

In spite of the pain that shot through her leg when she moved, she sat up and looked over the edge of her trench, trying to make out Slimane in the darkness.

"Slimane!"

Could he be sleeping that soundly?

The animal (for it was certainly an animal—a hyena or a jackal) was still there. Simmy could sense that it was crawling around nearby, hidden in the shadows. It was waiting for just the right moment, for her to show some sign of weakness, and it would pounce.

"Slimane!"

The shout seemed lost in the cold silence of the desert. She had the impression that her voice was not carrying, that the night had set up a wall, only a few yards away, to block it.

"Slimane!"

She wasn't calling now, but begging, pleading.

"Slimane!"

58

Then it struck her that he might have fled. How could he possibly have decided to betray her like this?

"Slim . . ." And she began to sob.

Soon, though, the instinct of self-preservation renewed her willpower, and she managed to sit up by hooking her arms over the edge of the trench. Then, beneath her fingers . . . what was that?

She groped through the sand and finally found the object she had felt for a second and then lost: a knife!

And then her canteen, and the biscuits! And Slimane's jacket! So he hadn't abandoned her after all! He couldn't be far. He had also left the rifles and the ammunition.

Now she regained her composure.

The thing to do, of course, was to chase away the animal.

She loaded one of the rifles, aimed at what she thought to be the position of the prowling beast, and pulled the trigger.

The report was followed by a long,

drawn-out howl, and then the sound of a swift, padded gallop across the slope of the dune.

Saved!

Simmy was so overcome by triumph and joy that she even forgot the pain of her wound.

But the excitement had made her very thirsty. She picked up the canteen and, without thinking, emptied it in one long draft. The cool water felt good on her hot, dry throat. Calmer now, she reloaded the gun; and, determined to defend herself against the wild animal if it reappeared, propped the gun against her knees and waited for Slimane's return.

❖   ❖   ❖

Slimane was struggling and out of breath. The bottle and the knapsack grew heavier with every step he took. In spite of everything, though, he was making progress.

60

He had decided on two stops when he started back to Simmy. Only two. And he wasn't going to make any more.

He looked up at the sky. The night was still very black, the day still far away.

He smiled. He could make it. He would arrive before dawn, just the way he had planned. Simmy would not learn of his absence until she woke up in the morning.

How much farther was it? Surely less than a mile.

Even though he had slowed down, the rhythm of his strides remained steady. He forgot about his fatigue and the crushing weight on his shoulders.

He was happy. He tried not to think how dry his throat felt, or how hungry he was. He concentrated on seeing Simmy again, on the good news he was bringing her, on the food, and on the nearly full bottle.

But he was very tired, and the load on his back was very heavy. His breath came unevenly. A voice kept whispering in his ear: "Come on, Slimane! You can take an-

61

other rest. Just a short one. Sit down and relax a few minutes. What's the difference? Ten little minutes!"

Slimane kept going. The voice continued, "Why are you making yourself suffer so? Don't you want to rest a while?"

"Slimane!"

That cry wasn't part of his imagination. It was very real.

"Slimane!"

That was Simmy shouting! And it sounded like a call for help! Even though her voice was muffled by the distance, it was easily recognizable.

Slimane strained his ears. There was no other noise to disturb the calm of the dark night, except the furious pounding of his heart. A cold sweat began to trickle down his bare chest.

Suddenly the crack of a rifle shot pierced the night.

VI

The Wild Animal

As soon as Slimane heard the shot all doubt vanished. He leaped forward. The weight of the bottle and the knapsack seemed of no consequence, and the voice that he had heard whispering in his ear was silent.

He scrambled wildly over the dunes. At last he found himself facing the slope with the vague silhouette of the bushes on top where Simmy . . .

❄   ❄   ❄

It was not Slimane's footsteps that alerted Simmy, for they were muffled by the sand, but his heavy, rapid panting. Then she saw him appear at the top of the dune. He collapsed as he reached her.

Two shapeless objects dropped next to him as he fell, but she didn't bother looking to see what they were.

Without even thinking about the burning pain in her leg, Simmy reached over and took him by the shoulders. He let himself be drawn to her and, leaning forward, dropped his head against her chest.

She put her arms around him and held him as if he were a child. She felt that he was damp with sweat and, afraid he would catch cold, she covered him with the tent-cloth.

      ✿   ✿   ✿

Slimane was still resting in the same position when the sun came up.

Simmy didn't dare make the slightest move, as she was afraid of disturbing his sleep.

Now it was daylight, and she could recognize the things he had brought with him, the goatskin bottle and the knapsack. Suddenly she understood why he had left the night before.

Her eyes filled with tears at the thought of her companion's devotion. The drops rolled down her cheeks and fell onto Slimane's face.

"Are you crying?" he asked.

She hadn't realized that he was awake.

She looked down at him. He smiled back up at her without moving. Impulsively, she leaned over and planted a large kiss on the middle of his forehead.

✿　✿　✿

Slimane helped her out of the trench and propped her up with her back against the edge of the dune. He held the bottle up to her lips.

"Drink, Simmy."

Simmy suddenly remembered what she had done that night, after her fright over the wild animal. She could see herself draining the canteen without thinking of her companion. If Slimane hadn't gone to get his water bottle, how would they manage without water all day? What would become of them without this precious bottle he was offering her before drinking himself?

Filled with remorse, she confessed to Slimane what she had done. Now it seemed to her that it had been the same as stealing. She was so upset that Slimane reassured her with a generous lie. He threw back his head and laughed.

"There was nothing wrong with what you did," he said. "There was hardly any water left, anyway. I admire you for having been satisfied with just those few miserable drops. The minute I laid hands on my water bottle I drank and drank and drank."

To make Slimane happy, Simmy pretended to take a few swallows. When she was finished, he drank, although he had to be very careful to restrain his longing to quench the fire in his throat. He figured that the water might be indispensable to Simmy. Her wounds would have to be washed. And he thought it might be a good idea for her to clean herself up a bit—her hands and, in particular, her face, which was sticky with sweat and patches of sand.

As for him, he was used to a rougher life; he could wait. It wasn't that he enjoyed being dirty, but today . . . and besides . . . a girl owes it to herself to look pretty, while a man . . .

With this gallant thought, he lit a fire of twigs and used it to heat the mixture of cornmeal and water he made in Simmy's mess-tin.

It wasn't long before the mixture was ready, but all of a sudden Slimane realized that they didn't have any salt. Cornmeal mush without salt? No sooner had this thought occurred to him than he remembered that they didn't have any forks or spoons, either. Only his knife.

Slimane hesitated, embarrassed to present Simmy with the mush under such primitive eating conditions. If only he had even one fork and a spoon!

He finally made up his mind to tell her what was troubling him. When she heard, she burst out laughing.

"Salt? So what? A fork and spoon? What in the world does all that matter? Our ancestors used their fingers. Come on, Slimane, I'm hungry as a bear."

Bewildered, he handed her the mess-tin.

She plunged her hand into it and rolled a portion of the mush into a ball. She squeezed it to make it firmer, put it into her mouth, and then chewed and swallowed. Her face lit up, and she reached out quickly for more.

Slimane watched her, astounded.

"Hurry up!" she warned him with her mouth full. "I can easily gobble up all of your share if you sit around waiting. I've never tasted anything so good in my whole life!"

❖   ❖   ❖

Slimane pitched the tent, using some branches he had cut down and stuck in the sand. The shelter would afford an excellent protection against the burning heat of the sun. In the evening he would take the canvas down and use it to cover Simmy as he had done the night before.

When the tent was ready he asked to see her wounds. They looked clean enough, but he still thought it wise to wash them with boiled water. He decided to do the same thing every day until they had healed.

While he was taking care of Simmy's leg, he thought back over the events of the night before. First exhaustion and sleep, and then the work he had been doing since he had awakened, had kept him from questioning her earlier. He asked, "What was it you fired at last night? Another Egyptian lighting a cigarette?"

She pouted. "Nasty!"

"Simmy! Look, I was only joking," he reproached her. "You don't have to worry about my feelings for you. You're like a sister."

A sister! The word both surprised and reassured her.

"I'm sorry; I was being silly."

She told him about her adventure. Slimane was skeptical.

"Are you sure you didn't dream it?"

"Oh, Slimane!" she protested.

He insisted: "With women you can never tell!"

Simmy decided to laugh it off. "Maybe you're right. Now that I think of it, I seem to remember seeing an Egyptian in my sleep."

"Ah! There you are."

"But he wasn't what I shot at."

"Liar!" he teased.

"He looked like you, Slimane."

Her voice was tender, and her eyes shone.

❖　❖　❖

After they had eaten, they took stock of their meager supplies.

By eating cornmeal one morning and bread the next, and chewing on biscuits at night, they would be able to hold out for a week. But even with very careful rationing, the water would be gone in half that time.

"The situation isn't quite desperate," concluded Slimane, "but it's not exactly anything to rejoice about."

Simmy could detect a note of discouragement in his voice. Very carefully she went over all the provisions again.

But the result was the same: one week's worth of food. As for water . . .

Simmy was overcome by despair. She felt somehow that she was responsible.

"If I hadn't . . ." she began.

"What do you mean?" he asked, after a pause.

"If I hadn't fired at you . . ."

"Then what?"

"We wouldn't be in this situation."

"You're mad, Simmy!"

"Oh, Slimane!"

He mimicked her contrite look.

"And if I hadn't decided to light a cigarette! If I hadn't struck the match!"

"Slimane, I—" He interrupted her: "We would still be hating each other. And we wouldn't have the pleasure we're getting out of knowing each other."

Suddenly worried, he asked: "But maybe you don't feel the same way?"

"Oh, Slimane!"

It was uttered with such sincerity that he was totally reassured.

❖ ❖ ❖

Slimane was sleeping.

"The animal!"

At her cry, he gave a start and was on his feet in a single bound.

"There!" Simmy shouted, pointing toward the south.

Not quite awake yet, he looked in the direction she was pointing. He had to shield his eyes with his hand because, although the tent blocked the sun's rays, it didn't lessen the reflection of light on the dunes.

"There! There!" repeated Simmy, in great excitement.

He could just see a motionless gray head at the level of one of the dunes. He watched it a moment and then lay down again without showing the slightest sign of alarm.

"Well," said Simmy, astonished at his indifference. "Is that all you're going to do?"

Yawning, he murmured, "It's a dog."

VII

Happy Days

In the west, the sun was touching the horizon. Dusk would shortly be falling on the desert.

Suddenly the silhouette of the animal rose into view. Simmy couldn't hide her fright. "Are you sure it's a dog?"

Slimane sighed, shrugged, and answered: "I've already told you so."

"Poor creature!"

"Yes, poor creature."

"He's in the same situation we're in."

"Almost. Except that we have provisions."

"And there isn't anything we can do for him?"

"Yes, there is."

"What?"

"Put an end to his suffering."

"Oh, no, Slimane!"

"Obviously it's a rather cruel solution."

"It certainly is!"

"I can't say I like the idea. But the dog may well be dangerous. I wouldn't dream of leaving you alone with him around."

"You mean you're planning to . . ."

"I have to return to the battleground by tomorrow night if we want to stay alive."

"Slimane! We have food for a week and water for four days. Can't you wait a couple of days? Maybe the dog will decide to go away."

"No. He's hungry and, more than anything, thirsty. We represent salvation to him. If we don't do something about him, he'll get bolder. Pretty soon he'll become crazed, violent. He'll attack us."

"If that happens, we can defend ourselves."

"During the daytime he'll move so

quickly that we can't be sure of hitting him. And at night . . ."

"What are we going to do, Slimane?"

He could tell she was trembling with fear.

"There just might be another solution," he murmured thoughtfully.

He emptied the knapsack of everything it held. Then, carrying it and the goatskin bottle, he walked toward the dog, which was standing motionless, watching them from a dune.

"Why don't you take a gun with you?" Simmy suggested, seeing that he had nothing to defend himself with.

Slimane kept on going without answering her.

When he had covered half the distance between the tent and the dog, he stopped and dug a hole in the ground. He placed in it the waterproof knapsack, which molded itself to the shape of the hole. He poured some of the water from the bottle into the improvised basin and walked slowly and calmly back toward Simmy.

He had hardly reached the tent when the dog rushed to the water.

"Tomorrow morning," Slimane said, "I'll move the basin nearer. I'll also put a little of the mush out with the water. Maybe I'll be able to tame him before we run out of food—that is, if he hasn't already gone completely wild from what he's had to go through."

Night came quite suddenly.

Slimane fell asleep right away.

Simmy lay awake for a while, looking up at the stars twinkling in the dark sky.

✼　　✼　　✼

The next day, Slimane took the improvised basin and set it down, along with the food, only twenty paces from where they were camped.

The dog moved about on the crest of

the dune as Slimane arranged the water and food. When Slimane had gone, the dog first sniffed the place where the knapsack had been the evening before, and then, instead of rushing toward the bait, as they had expected, he hesitated, turning in circles, sniffing the air, all the while keeping his eyes fixed on Simmy and Slimane.

"How can we get him to trust us?" whispered Simmy.

"By not moving," murmured Slimane. "And especially by not raising our voices when he comes near."

In spite of his indirect approach and frequent stops, the dog gradually neared his goal.

Simmy and Slimane never took their eyes off him.

Even though his ribs showed and his coat was dull, he was still a superb animal. He held his head high. His ears turned, trembled, at the slightest sound.

Five yards from the hole he became

doubly cautious. He watched the two of them intently, and he seemed to be encouraged by their stillness.

He came closer and closer, finally reaching the hole.

He drank, tentatively at first and then in large gulps. Next he turned to the mush, which he gulped down even faster than the water.

Simmy couldn't hold back her joy.

"It's going to work, Slimane!"

The cry alarmed the dog. He jumped sideways and landed on trembling paws. He pointed his muzzle toward them.

"Sh!" Slimane breathed.

The dog came back to the mush and finished off the last bit. Then, satisfied, he turned round and trotted off, looking back every so often. Once he even stopped and turned round. Slimane then spoke to him gently.

The dog showed no sign of fear. He lay down on the sand, wagging his tail, and stared at their little camp.

"I'm positive," Simmy said delightedly, "that you'll be able to stroke him soon."

"At what price!" Slimane sighed, gauging the water in the bottle with a worried look.

*   *   *

Simmy had been right. Later that day Slimane did manage to stroke the dog. But he still refused to follow Slimane.

It wasn't until evening, just a little before nightfall, that Slimane got him to come over to the tent, As for Simmy, the dog adopted her the minute she offered it a biscuit.

"You see, Slimane," she announced triumphantly, "a good deed is never wasted."

"Yes," he agreed, and added, half-serious, half-joking, "but the water and the cornmeal and the biscuits, all that is lost for good!"

His remark made Simmy think of how

hard it would be for Slimane to feed a third mouth.

She admitted sadly, "You're right. I think too much about myself. I'm selfish. Again, I only thought of what I wanted. I tell you what to do without ever thinking about the consequences or about the trouble it's going to be for you."

Slimane watched her with an ironic smile.

She continued: "And then you do what I ask. I'm just taking advantage of how good you are."

Suddenly, upset by Slimane's mocking expression, she almost shouted: "Aren't you going to say anything? Defend yourself! Say something!"

Slimane stopped smiling. He answered very seriously: "You're so silly. How can you doubt my friendship? I'm happy to do what you ask."

Simmy began to cry. Slimane put a comforting hand on her shoulder. The dog seemed to misinterpret this gesture, for he growled and showed his teeth.

"Bravo!" Slimane exclaimed. "Our new friend is ready to defend you, if necessary. I can leave you in his care without any worry."

It was almost night.

Slimane deftly lined the bottom of Simmy's trench with hot coals and covered them with sand, as he had done before. He took down the tent-cloth and, after installing Simmy in her warm bed, tucked it round her.

"See you tomorrow, Simmy!"

And he set off, disappearing into the dusk.

❁   ❁   ❁

By eleven o'clock he had reached the bombed trucks.

Among the thousands of things destroyed or scattered by the battle, he found (as he had expected) some canned food and some jerricans filled with water.

First he carried one jerrican to a place halfway between the battleground and their camp, and buried it there. Then he returned to the battleground and loaded himself with all sorts of provisions, some utensils that were absolutely necessary, three tent-cloths, two blankets, and a small medical kit. On the way back to their camp he buried half of the food next to the reserve water, and continued on his way with the rest.

He got back to Simmy at dawn.

He did the same thing for the next two nights. After the eight hours of exhausting work each night, he had to sleep in the daytime.

When he had finished, he was well satisfied.

Between what he had brought back and the store of provisions buried near the camp,

Simmy and he and even the dog had enough supplies to last at least two weeks.

* * *

The things Slimane had chosen made life much more comfortable for these two Robinson Crusoes of the desert.

They now had forks and spoons, plates, and aluminum cups. They built a fire in a hollow dug in the sand, and over it placed an iron tripod holding a saucepan for heating their food.

Their meals were appetizing, thanks to the variety of the canned food Slimane had found.

They fixed the four tent-cloths on telescoping poles made especially for this sort of thing. This provided good protection against the chill of the night. The blankets kept Simmy warm enough at night so that Slimane no longer had to make her a bed of embers.

As soon as it was morning, they opened

the two opposite flaps of the tent and thus let in a welcome flow of air.

Simmy's wounds were clean and seemed to be healing over well, thanks to the sulfa drugs and the sterile dressings found in the medical kit.

Simmy began to walk, and the pain that had once stopped her every time she tried to take a step had now disappeared entirely.

"In a few days," Slimane told her, "you'll be able to cover the short distance to the 'reserve'."

VIII

Memories Erased by Suffering

They had decided to move on. The previous night Slimane had carried many things to the site of their new camp. Although he was quite sure that Simmy would be able to cover the distance in two or three hours, he had thought it wise to move most of their possessions beforehand, so that he would be free to help her if necessary. He had kept provisions for two days, two tent-cloths, and one gun.

The sun was setting. The evening shadows were lying toward the east. A low breeze brushed the sands.

"Ready?" asked Slimane.

"Yes," answered Simmy. She stood up.

"Perhaps I could carry something?" she suggested, seeing Slimane throwing the gun, the bundles, and the goatskin bottle over his shoulder.

"No," he answered. "Think about your wounds—they've only just closed."

"But . . ."

Slimane cut short the argument. "Let's go!" he said.

❋   ❋   ❋

The dog led the way, his nose to the ground, walking in the tracks Slimane had made going back and forth between the camp and the "reserve."

The boy followed the dog, a few yards ahead of Simmy. Often he turned and asked: "Are you all right?"

She reassured him: "Fine, Slimane!"

The shadows had disappeared. They were making only slow progress—too slow. Slimane found his load growing heavy. He bent further forward and shifted his burdens by a quick movement of his shoulder. But this gave him only temporary relief. His back soon started to ache again. To help himself forget this, he asked again: "Still all right, Simmy?"

"Yes, thanks."

He struggled on, slightly comforted, and decided not to speak again for three minutes.

"You're not tired, Simmy?"

"No, I'm fine."

He loved the sound of her voice! After a few moments, he realized that he was asking more frequent questions.

"Your leg?"

"It's doing what I ask of it."

He became aware that he was moving less quickly. His calves were still going strong and his feet were steady, but his back seemed about to break. More than ever he felt the need to drown his fears in a flood of words. But what was there to say? He had already asked innumerable times if Simmy was all right. Wouldn't he communicate his anxiety to her if he continued to ask questions? Would he not betray the fact that he himself was close to exhaustion?

But one thing he was sure of: he mustn't stop. They must escape from the hell of Sinai, whatever the cost. This was only the first step toward the battlefield, the road, toward liberty and life.

So, as long as Simmy didn't ask to rest...

✻　✻　✻

Slimane stumbled, and his train of thought was broken.

"Only a couple of miles more, Simmy," he said encouragingly.

There was no answer.

"Simmy!"

Silence. He turned round. Simmy had disappeared! So had the dog! Slimane called her name. His cries were swallowed up by the night. Anxiously he took off his load and retraced his steps. Finally he caught sight of them both, scarcely visible in the darkness:

Simmy was lying along their tracks, her face on the ground, and the dog was sitting by her feet. When Slimane bent down, the dog growled. Slimane calmed him, seized Simmy, and set her up. Allah be praised! Her heart was beating!

His hand stroked the girl's face, his fingers removing the grains of sand that were sticking to the corners of her lips, to her nostrils, and along the edges of her closed eyelids. Ceaselessly, gently, he murmured to her.

At last Simmy made an almost imperceptible movement and opened her eyes. Slimane was filled with joy.

But what a strange resurrection! When Simmy regained consciousness, she immediately began to heap reproaches upon him!

Slimane couldn't believe his ears.

"Be quiet!" he managed to whisper at last, thoroughly frightened.

"Why should I be quiet? No, Slimane, you are going to hear me out. You are going to listen to me. You could have put me out of my misery. That would have been the action of a soldier. But to save me only to desert me afterward, that's what I call cowardice. When I think that I believed in your friendship, and that you said you were my brother!"

"Simmy!"

"I forbid you to use my name."

"Simmy!"

"Stop it, I tell you. There's nobody who is Simmy to you any more." Then she suddenly ceased her accusations.

Had she exhausted her arguments, or was she lucid again? Slimane didn't know what to think. Was she crazed by fever? or by pain? Perhaps her wounds had opened again. He wished he could persuade her to let him examine them. But he didn't dare to ask her.

Simmy began to speak again, her breath coming quickly: "Soon you'll be back with your companions. You'll be able to tell them about your victory. You'll laugh, you'll make fun of my naiveté, all of you. No, of my stupidity! Because I believed in you. What madness! To trust the word of the most vile being in the whole world."

Then, her voice hoarse with fury, she added the last, terrible insult: "An Egyptian!"

Slimane clenched his teeth at this outrage. What could he do? How could he bring her back to reason? How could he show her that she was talking nonsense? that there was no truth in the accusation she was leveling at him? that, on the contrary, he was still ready to sacrifice himself so that she could live?

"An Egyptian!" she repeated with the same violence.

Slimane was in despair. Why had Allah helped him only to abandon him in the end in these terrible circumstances?

"An Egyptian! An Egyptian!"

Simmy shattered the quiet night with these words which she continued to repeat with an intonation that grew ever crueler and more scornful.

"An Egyptian!"

Her voice carried all the hostility of one people for another, all the bitterness that had accumulated through the centuries.

"Allah!" prayed Slimane from the depths of his distress, "why do you allow this enmity to soil our friendship—the first, the only lovely thing in my miserable life?"

"An Egyptian!"

Tirelessly, Simmy reminded him of the uselessness of his efforts to understand, his attempts to be kind.

"An Egyptian!"

Suddenly Slimane rebelled. He had listened to her for too long already. Why, and for whom, had he gone to such trouble and endured so much? At last he burst out: "Shut up, Jew!"

At once he regretted his moment of weakness. But how distant their happy times together seemed now! It was as if they had smashed them to pieces.

What should he do now? If Simmy was

lost to him forever, he would rather die than survive without her friendship.

Slowly, he walked to the place where he had dropped his load. In a few moments he came back. Simmy was watching him warily.

"Egyptian!" she spat at him.

He knelt in front of her and offered her the butt of his rifle. She took it, and pointed the gun right at Slimane's throat. Calm now, he murmured, his voice low but steady: "I want you to be happy. Destroy me if you must. Allah and your God will know that I die of my own free will. Go on, Simmy, fire! Kill the Egyptian you hate."

The gun fell against his chest. He closed his eyes . . .

IX

Reconciliation

Simmy felt the cold of the steel penetrate
her fingers. Her whole body shivered. What
was this she was holding? A gun? Why?
Was she dreaming?

No. She could see it was night. She became aware of the dog beside her. Why
was she on her knees? What an atrocious
headache she had! How her wounds hurt!
And where was she?

She dropped the gun and groped round
her on the sand. No provisions, no goatskin
bottle. Nothing. The darkness hid Slimane
from her.

Gradually she came to her senses. She
remembered.

She remembered setting out for the "reserve" at dusk. She remembered their slow progress. She saw Slimane ahead of her, bent under the weight of a heavy load. She was advancing with difficulty. She had slowed down and fallen behind Slimane. Soon she lost sight of him. Fear had overcome her. Her legs had refused to carry her any farther. She had struggled, become exhausted, fallen to the ground . . .

How clearly she remembered that instant! Her pride had prevented her from confessing her exhaustion to her friend when he had asked if she was tired.

Friend?

She recalled clearly her inexplicable revulsion. Slimane had become her enemy again! What was the matter with her? She remembered her sudden hatred, and the wild accusations she had made against him. She could hear herself hurling insults at him.

Horrorstruck, she thought of the gun she had pointed at him, of her readiness to kill him. How could she have done it? And what use were regrets now? What good were her tears? Would Slimane forgive her if he knew how sorry she was? Would he ever again be able to believe in her sincerity? Never, she thought bitterly. Appalled at her infamous conduct, she cried out, in despair, "Forgive me, Slimane!" and sobbed heartbrokenly.

Suddenly she found herself in his arms. Gently he stroked her as he kept repeating: "It's all right, Simmy. It's all right. You were just delirious from exhaustion and the wounds."

❋　❋　❋

At dawn they reached the "reserve." Slimane had dragged Simmy, crouching on a piece of canvas, across the dunes. He had made detours round the crests, doubling the distance they had to travel. The dog had trudged along slowly and painfully. It had taken four hours to complete a journey that should have taken half that time. Four hours, during which he had been harnessed like a beast of burden to this square of rough, waterproof material, which had made his hands raw. Four hours of struggling, which had brought him almost to breaking point, so that frequently he had thought he would be incapable of reaching their destination. During all those hours, not a word had passed between them. But now as daylight approached they had at last arrived.

They had turned their backs on each other. Simmy was ashamed and embarrassed and thought Slimane was angry. Neither of them fully trusted that moment of reconciliation before they set out. She didn't even dare to tell him again how sorry she was. And Slimane was afraid she still hadn't completely come to her senses. He even hesitated to reassure her that he was still her friend.

The sun came up. Soon, if they didn't protect themselves from its rays, they would be in danger. He must do something before it was too late. He turned toward her and held out his arms: "Simmy!"

"Slimane!"

❉   ❉   ❉

Slimane pitched the tent. Thus protected from the sun, they ate and fed the dog, who promptly went to sleep in a corner of the tent. Slimane rebandaged Simmy's leg. Then, lying beside each other in the tent, they tried to understand how the hatred they thought had been driven out of their hearts forever had surged up again so horribly as the result of a trivial incident.

"I prayed to Allah," said Slimane.

"Perhaps, in a way, I prayed to my God, too," said Simmy.

"Do you think they were deaf to our prayers? They did not help us."

"What do you mean, Slimane?"

"I wonder whether they really exist."

"Oh, Slimane, that's blasphemy! You're letting anger blind you."

"On the contrary, I think I may have made a discovery."

"What have you discovered?"

"How many religions are there?"

"I don't know exactly, but there are certainly many."

"Listen, Simmy! Since every religion claims that its god is the true god, isn't it logical to suspect that they're all mistaken?"

"Do you know the parable of the rings?"

"No, I've never heard of it."

"Then listen, Slimane, and I'll tell you. A merchant on his deathbed had his three sons brought to him. He said to them: 'My children, I have nothing to leave you except these three rings. One of them is a talisman. It will bring happiness and riches to whoever possesses it. Unfortunately, I've mixed them up, and, as they all look the same, I don't know which is the magic one.' Each of the boys took one of the gold rings and went out into the world. Some years later, they met in their native land at the tomb of their old father. All three of them had been very successful in everything they had tried to do. What do you make of that?"

"All three rings were magic!" exclaimed Slimane.

"No," said Simmy.

"Well, then, I don't understand."

"Not one of them, in fact, was a magic ring."

"But then . . ."

"Each of the boys was convinced that he had the magic ring. They believed this without proof and succeeded in all their ventures. In other words, they had faith."

The word struck Slimane. He repeated slowly: "They had faith . . ."

"Yes, Slimane. All religions are to be respected. We shouldn't set one against the other. Do they not, all of them, without exception, teach us to love our neighbor? What does it matter whether they teach it in Arabic, or Hebrew, or any other language?"

"You're right, Simmy. Our religions do teach us to help each other, and not to quarrel over differences. So we must only fight in future to destroy the real enemy: hatred. Simmy, when we get back, tell these truths to your people, and I will tell them to my brothers, when we find them again."

Simmy looked at him with affection. How handsome he was, she thought, when he was speaking with such excitement.

X

Destiny Strikes

For three days they had been enjoying the pleasure of living off the "reserve." The cans of food Slimane had buried here provided them with a variety of dishes. Since they were only an hour's walk from the battle-ground, where they could get more provisions when they needed them, they were able to eat and drink as much as they wanted.

Every day Slimane made a trip to what he jokingly called "the larder." They no longer felt afraid when they thought of themselves as Robinson Crusoes of the desert. Without admitting it to each other, they thought, not without some sadness, of the coming separation, which would put an end to their adventures as well as to their friendship. Each of them felt secretly that he would willingly prolong this isolation from which they were deriving great pleasure.

They spoke, often, of their last quarrel, but only to laugh about it and to reiterate to each other that it had only bound them closer together. After one of these conversations, Simmy said: "I know that exhaustion and fear get you into a state of nerves where you do stupid things. But I won't be like that again."

Cautiously, Slimane amended that by saying: "Don't be too sure. Does one ever know?"

"What are you afraid of?"

"I don't know. Perhaps you won't really be in control of your nerves when they are tested again."

"I'm sure I won't be like that again! I've thought about it many times. I know I won't get angry again."

"I admire your self-confidence. I couldn't be so sure of myself."

Simmy looked at him thoughtfully before speaking again.

"If you should have a breakdown like the one I had, I'd remember how you helped me, and I'd help you to get over it."

*　*　*

The day had been hot and airless. It remained warm and heavy even when the sun had gone down. There was no breeze to freshen the first part of the night as there had been on previous evenings.

Neither Simmy nor Slimane could sleep. The dog, too, was ill at ease. He went out of the tent, wandered around, came back, lay down again, got up, went out again. His behavior attracted their attention, and he became the subject of their conversation.

"We haven't given him a name yet," said Simmy.

"No," agreed Slimane, astonished.

"What do you suggest?" continued Simmy.

107

"Oh, I really don't know," answered the boy, laughing. "Give me a chance to think."

"I'm only asking you for a name."

"I can't think of one. What about you? What do you suggest?"

"I'm trying to think. I'd like something original—something that would remind us of our adventure and our meeting."

"Sinai!"

"Yes, that's marvelous!" cried Simmy. "On the Sinai desert we have had misfortune and joy, disappointments and hopes. Adopted!"

They decided to have the dog immediately to answer to his name. After a little while the animal, who was intelligent, understood what they expected of him. They got a lot of amusement out of making him do various things. Then, suddenly, an unusual noise interrupted them.

"It's an engine," suggested Simmy.

"An airplane engine," said Slimane, more precisely.

He rushed out of the tent and threw some of their stock of branches onto the dying embers of the fire. Simmy joined him.

"What are you doing?"

Pausing, Slimane explained: " I want to signal that we're here."

The thick smoke didn't seem to bother him. He didn't come out of it until he had seen the flames attack the branches and make a large circle of light. The humming of the engine grew louder and louder. There could be no doubt: it was certainly an airplane, and it was coming in their direction. The pilot must have seen the fire. Of course, he couldn't land near them in the middle of the night. But he had spotted them. Slimane couldn't conceal his joy. The plane—whatever its nationality, Israeli or Egyptian—would surely give the alarm. One side or the other would know that there were living beings in the nightmarish desert of Sinai. And the next day, at daybreak . . .

❊   ❊   ❊

But the next day, when daybreak came, Slimane didn't know it until the warmth of

109

the sun made him realize that the night had passed. Perhaps he would never again see the dawn. He sat with his head on his knees, unable to see any ray of light. He was blind!

He kept his eyes closed for long periods, and then opened them, slowly, after massaging them with his fingers. Each time he could see only darkness.

"Slimane!" murmured Simmy.

"Shut up!"

Simmy's voice, the voice he had loved so much, was no help at all; in fact, it exasperated him. He remembered everything he had done for her since they had first met. He regretted all of it. He blamed her for all their misfortunes, for all his own misfortunes. If only he had never met her! If he hadn't helped her! Then he'd have reached Bir el Rakaba. Perhaps he would even be among his own pople in Cairo by now! Yes, certainly, he would be in Cairo. The barracks of El Gombouria! Real meals! A decent bed!

"Slimane!" murmured Simmy again.

"Cursed Jew!"

He continued with a long litany of insults, which did not appease his rancor. It was her fault that he was blind. Only an Israeli plane would have machine-gunned them like that.

Slimane remembered the diabolical attack: three low flights with bursts of tracer bullets riddling the night. By a miracle he and Simmy had not been hit. But during the final dive a sheaf of bullets had hit the fire, violently flinging burning embers mixed with sand into Slimane's eyes.

What could he do now? He would be better off dead. What was to become of him? He was at Simmy's mercy. What would she decide? It didn't matter, for he would accept nothing from her. She was the enemy!

"Slimane!"

"Shut up!" he growled, "or I'll . . ."

He stood up and groped his way toward her, his features contorted with rage.

Simmy remembered the words she had

spoken: "If you should have a breakdown like the one I had, I'd remember how you helped me, and I'd help you to get over it." As Slimane's hands reached for her throat, she went limp and made no move to escape.

XI

Wonderful Simmy

Slimane felt his anger die as his hands touched Simmy's slender neck. A wave of memories engulfed him, and suddenly the blackness seemed to lighten.

After saving Simmy from death before, should he kill her now? And the pleasure that caring for her had given him, those wonderful moments that had brought them so close? And the pride they had shared in overcoming their hatred and suspicion? Was he to forget all that now, erase it from his memory? No! Impossible!

Simmy's gesture of surrender, her willingness to let him strangle her, reminded him of something. He, too, had said to her one day as she held his rifle: "Go on, Simmy, fire! Kill the Egyptian you hate."

113

And she hadn't fired . . .

Slimane did not close his fingers round Simmy's neck. He couldn't. His hands fell to his sides. Suddenly he felt himself sway as his legs gave way beneath him.

"I must be out of my mind," he murmured, and dropped to the ground at her feet.

Simmy understood.

❖   ❖   ❖

Simmy had been nursing Slimane tirelessly for three days. She washed his eyes with compresses of boiled water, then used a few drops of some eye lotion she had found in the medical kit, and afterward covered the lids with a gauze bandage. The process was repeated several times a day and continued through the night.

Slimane bore up courageously, even though it upset him to be so entirely dependent on Simmy. From the moment he showed signs of wanting to move about, she had guided him wherever he wanted to go.

When the meals were ready, she would feed him as she would a child.

She was determined to do whatever she could to help him, never once complaining, and trying all the while to keep his hopes up.

"You'll get better, Slimane, I'm sure you'll get better," she would tell him over and over again.

She was so persuasive that Slimane was convinced it would not be long before he would be able to see again.

Yes, he would get better. Yes, he would come out of his night. Yes, he would once again be able to take pleasure in watching the sun shining down on everything round him.

He would come to life again.

He would be able to see Simmy again, her radiant face, her clear blue eyes, her smile.

He would tell her how grateful he was. He would tell her that he would never doubt her again, that from now on all the reasons for their quarreling were gone, that he wanted nothing more than to listen to her, to do whatever she wanted.

"The water!"

Simmy's voice startled him out of his thoughts. He heard her run out of the tent. He could hear the jerrican, then the goatskin bottle, being shaken. Worried, he called: "What's the matter?"

"Nothing," she answered.

But, determined as she was to remain calm, she couldn't keep the note of fear from her voice.

"Tell me the truth," he insisted.

"There's almost no water left."

      ✿   ✿   ✿

Simmy had gone. Slimane knew that night covered the desert.

By the light of the moon she would be able to follow the tracks he had made across the sand during his trips to the combat area. It would take her an hour to reach it. She would have no trouble getting there. But what about getting back? Would she know enough to take no more than four or five quarts of water? More than that would be too much for her limited strength.

Suddenly Slimane was struck with a terrible thought. Simmy had been working so hard for the last three days, suppose wounds on her leg had opened again, had even become infected?

She had devoted herself entirely to him, undoubtedly forgetting to take care of her leg, still not completely healed. She had taken on the responsibility of running the camp single-handed. She had prepared all the meals, fed the dog, taken care of the bedding and the guns. She had even managed to tidy up the tent each morning.

And now, understanding their need for water and aware that Slimane would not be able to travel until he had regained the use of his eyes, she had decided to go to the combat area herself.

The thought of Simmy's making that long hike with an injured leg made Slimane shudder. He wondered what this courageous action would cost her. Had it ever even occurred to her that she was running an enormous risk by putting so much strain on a leg that was not yet healed?

Slimane tortured himself with thoughts of the chance Simmy had taken. His hopes that they would soon be able to get out of the desert were overshadowed by his fear for Simmy. It was more than he could bear.

He could feel the tears forming in his eyes. They seeped through the light gauze and rolled down his cheeks.

❧   ❧   ❧

Simmy had arrived at the combat area. It was the first time she had actually seen the effects of war.

She stopped short, frozen with horror at the sight of the smashed vehicles and the debris strewn across the sand. The cold, bright light of the moon gave the scene a ghostly appearance and made the long shadows seem even blacker.

How many soldiers had died during the attack? Simmy knew that there had been many. She also knew that there must be corpses lying hidden in folds of the dunes that had been ripped up by the bombs.

Her brothers, the Israelis, were responsible for this horrifying chaos. Simmy was so shaken that it didn't even occur to her that the Egyptians had, in their turn, destroyed some of her own people.

She shuddered with pity and disgust. If only she need never look on another spectacle like this! She made up her mind to do everything in her power to prevent it from ever happening again.

True, she was only fourteen years old, but she would grow up. Nothing would get in the way of her mission. Nothing would stifle her voice.

Without regard for the race, religion, class, or rank of the killers, she would shout out the horror that a woman feels at their hideous death games.

She would gather thousands of mothers

119

behind her, of all nationalities, and they would refuse to offer their sons and brothers for the sacrifice.

No, never again could there be war.

If she was unable to complete her mission, she would leave the job to her children.

What was essential was to prepare the ground for life, not death. She had no illusions. Much time would pass before she, and those who aided her, would be able to break through the indifference and inertia.

But what did that matter?

The day would come when peace would be universal. It would be indestructible.

And then light and laughter and love would blossom, sweeping away the shadows and the tears and the hatred. That would be the happy time of which the prophets spoke. All the prophets.

✻　✻　✻

The resolutions Simmy had made helped her overcome her fears. With a firm, steady step, she made her way toward the dark hulks of the nearest vehicles, which stood out against the blue-black velvet of the night.

She had forgotten to ask Slimane where she would have the best chance of finding water.

She had already searched through a number of wrecks, two tanks, and three trailers, without any luck, when she became aware that a warm breeze was blowing. Strange! Until now the nights had always been cool.

To ward off her rising uneasiness, she concentrated on the reason for her coming to the battleground—water.

She noticed a truck overturned in a bomb crater. She slid down into the funnel-shaped hole to investigate. The cargo seemed to be intact. Groping in the darkness, she touched cases and bundles much too large to move.

She could tell by the sounds above that the breeze had by now become a wind.

Still groping, she continued her explorations: a large metal chest, bands of ammunition . . .

The gusts of wind were catching up the grains of sand and throwing them violently into the crater.

Simmy increased her efforts, her teeth gritting on the sand dust blown into her throat and lungs. But she would keep going. She had to find water!

Suddenly she came in contact with something smooth. It was flexible but firm, neither wood nor iron—a container made of plastic.

She carefully studied the shape with her fingers: a mold-mark . . . two crossed grooves . . . higher up, handles.

It was a jerrican! And it was full of water!

It was very hard for her to disentangle the precious jerrican from the pile of crates and cases surrounding it and then to drag it to the top of the crater.

But she felt great joy at having succeeded despite the squalls of wind and her exhaustion, despite the fact that her wounds had reopened and were beginning to bleed again.

Any thoughts of her own troubles, or of the risk she was taking, were blotted out by her overwhelming joy at having found water. More than fifteen quarts of water!

Her mission, however, was not yet quite accomplished. She still wanted to find some cigarettes to replenish Slimane's stock, which, she knew, would be used up by the following day.

Deliberately ignoring the wind, which had redoubled its violence, and the pain that was tearing at her leg, she went back into the crater.

XII

The Light

Slimane couldn't sleep. Simmy's departure had left him solitary and uneasy. And he knew he would not relax until he heard her voice again.

He lit a cigarette to kill time, waiting anxiously for her return. He was rationing his cigarettes carefully. There were only eight left in the last pack.

Why in Allah's name hadn't he thought of asking Simmy to bring him some more?

✿   ✿   ✿

The dog stirred outside the tent.

Simmy had made him stay behind, even though he had wanted to follow her.

"Sinai!" Slimane called.

Sinai came and lay beside Slimane, but

he still seemed on edge. Slimane could feel him trembling. He tried to calm him, but it did no good. The minute Slimane stopped stroking him, the dog moved away and stretched out next to the fire.

From time to time he growled.

Slimane had been born and raised close to nature, close enough to take it seriously when an animal acted strangely.

There was no doubt that Sinai was disturbed by something. But by what? Or by whom?

Had his senses warned him of some undefined danger that was imminent?

Slimane was still wondering what the trouble was when the first wind rose.

The dog came to him immediately.

So that was all it was—the wind!

Slimane closed the tent, sealing it up as tightly as possible.

Good old Sinai!

❖   ❖   ❖

Simmy was on her way back. She had been struggling for an hour against the gusts of south wind that were slowing her progress.

How far had she come? She couldn't tell. There was only one thing that mattered, and that was to keep going in the right direction. It was all the more important because the sand, blown by the wind, had partly covered the tracks leading to the camp.

Besides, she had to use every bit of will-power she had to keep moving in spite of the fierce gusts that buffeted her from side to side. She had to brace her muscles to keep from falling.

She had tried several different ways of carrying the jerrican: with her arm hanging down, on her shoulder, on her head, clutched to her chest. None of them was satisfactory. Eventually she resigned herself to alternating from one to another.

Her progress was broken by more and more frequent stops to rest.

Her nostrils and her mouth were filled with sand. She felt as if she were chewing crumbled glass.

Steadily the gusts gained in strength and duration, and soon she was caught up in what seemed to be a tornado. It was as if a gigantic hand had lifted entire dunes in the air and let them drop back on her.

She was slowed to a halt.

When she lifted her foot to take a step, she lost her balance. She staggered, and finally she set the jerrican down on the ground, crouching next to it and hanging on with both hands until the squall had passed. Time after time, she started out again, lurching, clenching her teeth, cursing the wind that was tormenting her.

Despite everything she went on, trying to be careful, as she shifted the jerrican from one hand to the other, not to lose or crush the two cartons of cigarettes she had hung from her belt.

Visibility was now reduced to less than a yard. There was no sense in continuing. Exhausted, she slumped to the ground, feeling only the futility of prolonging the struggle.

The sand, as it settled down around her, molded itself to the shape of her body. If she stayed like this, she would die!

Covering her eyes and mouth with her fingers, she began to move, rolling from side to side so that the shifting, shroud-like sand would not envelop her. The effort used up the last of her energy.

It seemed there was no way out of this hell.

The thought of Slimane tortured her: Slimane alone, Slimane blind. Now he, too, would surely perish. Slimane, her brother.

Suddenly the sound of a shot pierced through the howling of the wind and made her jump.

Was she nearer to camp than she had thought?

She dragged herself into a sitting position.

A soft pink glow lit the eddies of whirling sand that were dancing wildly across the dunes ahead of her.

Had Slimane lit a fire?

129

With a supreme effort she managed to get to her feet.

She started out again, dragging the jerrican, which bumped and scraped her ankles, fighting the furious wind, struggling through the dark toward the last, slender ray of hope: the pale, flickering glow that might at any moment disappear in the storm.

❊　❊　❊

After Sinai had returned, the squalls had grown more and more violent with every minute that passed. Slimane realized that these were not ordinary gusts of wind, which might soon pass. This was a simoon —a sandstorm peculiar to desert regions. He knew what that could mean—not because he himself had ever experienced one, but from the terrifying accounts that the nomads had given him.

He began to worry about Simmy again. What if she had already been on her way back from the battleground when the simoon had started?

He tried to reassure himself. "To get there and then look around for the water," he said to himself, "must have taken her at least an hour and a half. She might also have stopped to rest for a few minutes. Yes, of course, she must have rested when she got there, after that tiring walk across the sand. What's more, she probably had some trouble finding the water right away, in the dark. And she was going into that mess of tanks and wrecked trucks for the first time . . ."

Slimane managed to persuade himself that Simmy had not started the trip back before the simoon began to blow.

Besides, she would certainly be able to tell that this was no ordinary storm. There was a desert in Israel, too. Surely Simmy knew about the simoon.

"Yes, she must have stayed where she was," Slimane decided. "She probably took shelter in one of the trucks."

*　　*　　*

The gauze bandage on Slimane's eyes was damp and had begun to come loose. He decided to take it off rather than try to fix it. He rolled it up carefully and put it in a corner of the tent. He wondered if his movements had disturbed Sinai, for the dog growled.

"Don't worry, I've finished now," Slimane told him. "You must be patient. You must wait, just as I'm waiting."

But Sinai continued to growl. Suddenly he barked.

Slimane could tell that he had stood up and was trying to get out of the tent. Slimane opened the flap for him.

The dog ran out, barking ferociously.

After a moment the sound began to grow fainter. Apparently Sinai was moving away.

Slimane wondered what the dog's abrupt departure could mean. He had crawled out of the tent to call Sinai back when a series of howls provided the answer.

"Hyenas!" he whispered.

His fear made his throat so dry that he could barely pronounce the word. If they attacked him, how could he possibly defend himself? He couldn't even see.

In the distance, Sinai's furious barking could be heard over the sharp cries of the wild beasts, and Slimane was suddenly roused from his frightening thoughts.

The dog was fighting to save him!

❖ ❖ ❖

Sinai's barking had stopped.

All Slimane could hear was the howling of the hyenas.

Would they attack him next?

They must have already scented the camp.

How many were there? Ten? Fifteen? More?

How could he drive them off?

He was paralyzed with terror. No! He was not going to resign himself to such a fate! He was not going to die without putting up a fight! But how?

His knife? An absurd weapon under the circumstances.

His gun? But he was blind!

A sudden squall knocked him down. Even on his knees, with his hands on the ground, the force of the wind was so strong that he found it difficult to keep his balance.

His jaws, which had been clenched tight for so long, finally loosened. The sand blew into his mouth and throat, and he choked. He thought he was about to lose consiousness, when suddenly . . .

Was it possible? Had his spirit already left this world? Was it already wandering toward Allah's paradise?

For there, within reach of his hand, was

134

a twinkling red spot. Was it a piece of a broken star, knocked out of the sky by the storm? Was this a dream?

The wind was real enough, though. Then . . . could it be . . .

Slimane reached out quickly and caught hold of the glowing red spot, afraid that at any moment it might disappear. As he touched it, he let out a cry of triumph, in spite of the sudden burning pain in his hand.

"Fire!"

Yes, he had picked up an ember from the fire! He was not dead! He was not dreaming! He was alive! And he could see!

The simoon had revived the coals without scattering them, thanks to the narrowness and depth of the small fireplace. In a moment Slimane had filled it with everything burnable he could lay his hands on: wood, cloth, the cartons from the biscuits.

Then he noticed the gun. Why not fire a round of shots for sheer joy, just to celebrate? A round? No, one shot would be enough. It would be better to save the cartridges.

The shot rang out above the fiendish howling of the wind. It echoed back and forth across the dunes.

The fire caught and blazed. The leaping flames were so bright that Slimane had to look away. And over there, twenty yards away, against a background of darkness streaked with whirling sand, he saw the hyenas fleeing, frightened by the light.

XIII

Hope

The simoon had lasted three days.

This morning, for the first time, the air was calm and the sun shone.

Slimane wanted to forget the long, horrible hours after Simmy had returned. He wanted to forget his desperate struggle to protect them with the few simple objects available.

He wanted to remember only one thing: that they had survived, thanks to the water that Simmy had managed to carry as far as their camp.

He looked at her as she lay resting on the one tent-cloth that was left after the disaster. Her hollow eyes were closed, and her drawn face was smudged and dirty. Her hair was matted with sand.

The scabs of her wounds had opened. Slimane had also discovered some open sores on her legs and ankles, made by the jerrican she had refused to abandon.

He had cleaned and bandaged her legs without waking her. Between her efforts to reach the camp and the days and nights without sleep, she had finally collapsed entirely.

Slimane was careful not to make any noise that might disturb her healing rest. He decided to wait until later to search for cans of food and other objects that might be buried under the wind-blown sand.

He moved away and walked toward the little mound that rose over the place where he had buried Sinai.

Slimane remembered the words that Simmy had spoken when the dog adopted her: "A good deed is never wasted."

No, never.

The dog had died to save his life.

✿　✿　✿

A week passed.

Each night, Slimane went back to the combat area.

On his first trip he brought back tent-cloths and blankets to replace those carried away by the simoon.

Next he replenished the reserve of food and the store of water.

When this was done, the worst of their worries were over.

Simmy's appetite returned. Her wounds were well on their way to healing again.

Often Slimane caught her humming quietly to herself.

One evening after supper Slimane sat thinking about the moment when they would return to civilization.

"I think," he said, "that in another two weeks you'll be in good enough shape to move around without my help. We'll go to the battleground and, from there, to the road linking Akaba to Noueiba."

"That region is almost surely held by Israeli troops," Simmy said.

"So what? I'd only be a privileged prisoner, since I'm your friend."

"Prisoner?"

"I was joking, Simmy. I'm sure they wouldn't keep a fourteen-year-old boy as hostage. They would send me back to Egypt."

"I certainly hope so. Still . . ."

"Still what?"

"Do you really want to be rescued?"

"I want it for you, Simmy."

"For me?"

"You've been in the desert long enough. For your safety and your health, you must leave as soon as possible. My job is to get you back to your friends."

"Won't you regret leaving the Sinai just a little?"

"We've suffered too much here; I'd rather forget it."

"Really, Slimane?"

"Forgive me, Simmy. I'd like to forget the Sinai, but I will remember you until the day I die."

140

"Don't think about our being separated, Slimane—at least, not yet."

"Do you have any other ideas?"

"Perhaps. I'll tell you about them when the time comes," she answered with a mischievous smile.

* * *

That night Slimane had returned to the combat area to carry out the first part of the plan Simmy had thought up. He would look among the wreckage, perhaps in a truck less damaged than the others, for a radio transmitter that had been spared by the bombing.

Simmy had admitted that she didn't really know how to repair a transmitter, but she had watched her sister operate one often enough so that she felt she could probably get one to work if it hadn't suffered too much damage.

"But the equipment is Egyptian," Slimane had pointed out.

"Egyptian, Israeli! All these transmitters

are alike. A few dials, three or four knobs to turn . . ."

Even though he was somewhat skeptical, Slimane had set out on the search.

He looked through several vehicles, but nothing of interest caught his attention.

He wandered from one truck to another. None of them was equipped with a radio. And the sets in the tanks were all completely smashed.

Slimane was beginning to lose hope when he noticed a truck overturned in a bomb crater. It was the one (although he was not aware of this) from which Simmy had taken the jerrican of water.

He slid down into the crater and, with a flashlight he had picked up earlier in the wreckage, examined the truck's cargo.

The thin beam lit up the metal siding of the truck.

Allah be praised! Those bolts of lightning painted on the siding were the symbol designating radio equipment.

First he would have to dislodge the enormous chest from the cases and bundles that were wedging it in. Then he would have to get it open and see exactly what was inside.

Slimane set to work eagerly.

❊ ❊ ❊

How had the accident happened?

Had the truck moved, or had its load shifted?

Slimane had no idea.

He had been digging in the sand when suddenly there was a crash, and his legs were caught underneath a heap of crates. The weight didn't hurt him much because the crates were resting partially on the sand.

But how could he get out of this position? How could he free himself? He twisted around, flexed his muscles—all in vain. Finally he decided to stay perfectly still. By moving around he might provoke another crash of crates and boxes, and that would only make matters worse.

143

It would be best to wait. Simmy would certainly get worried and come looking for him soon. Yes, he was sure she would come.

❖　❖　❖

Simmy awoke at dawn.

She was surprised not to see Slimane, but she was not immediately alarmed.

She knew that he had been absolutely determined to find the equipment they needed. Still, it was taking much longer than either had expected.

Ten o'clock . . . noon . . . Slimane still had not returned. As the afternoon wore on and it began to get dark, Simmy became worried. She was sure something must have happened to him.

Hadn't he said, before leaving, "I'll be back before dawn"?

Had he been overcome by exhaustion? Had he been forced to rest?

But no, that was impossible! Slimane was a pillar of strength.

144

What was keeping him, then? An accident?

She had to go and find him! In no time at all Simmy had made ready to leave the camp.

She bitterly regretted having asked Slimane to go back to the battlefield to look for a radio transmitter; it seemed such a foolish idea now!

As she stood up, she gave a cry of pain. Her leg still hurt very badly. But Slimane needed her!

She set off, limping, chanting to the rhythm of her steps: "Slimane . . . Slimane . . . Slimane . . ."

❋ ❋ ❋

She had finally succeeded in what had at first seemed impossible—extracting Slimane from the dangerous position he was in without bringing down more of the boxes and crates precariously perched on the truck.

145

Slimane hadn't been able to help her at all. She had worked alone, all through the night. She had removed tons of sand. She had shifted innumerable crates and bundles, using a shovel and a jack. Digging here, lifting there, she had carefully considered each step ahead of time to avoid making a false move that might bury him beyond hope of rescue.

Finally Slimane had been able to free his legs and wriggle out. He was bruised but alive.

They were resting now, sitting side by side on the comfortable seats in the cab of a truck.

Neither of them spoke, but they were both filled with a quiet joy. In spite of their fatigue, their faces shone, and they smiled at each other as they sat with clasped hands.

✻   ✻   ✻

The following day, when they at last pried open the metal chest that had caused them both so much pain and effort, their happiness was complete. Inside was a radio transmitter, and with it a great number of batteries, all still in good condition.

Simmy had quickly examined it, figured out how to operate it, and made sure that it was in working order.

"Look," Simmy explained, "I'm not going to use the signaling key, for I don't know the Morse code. But I've plugged in the microphone and we can talk into it. I've fixed it so that we'll be broadcasting on the international wavelength for S.O.S. calls. That way we'll stand a better chance of having our messages picked up."

They had agreed on the text of the messages they would send out in turn, he in Arabic and she in Hebrew.

She pulled down a lever.

The needles on the dials jumped. The speaker crackled.

Simmy and Slimane looked at each other, their faces flushed with excitement.

Now, at last, the long-awaited moment had come!

XIV

To End All War

But nothing seemed to happen for a long time.

Over and over they repeated their calls.

Then, suddenly, a confusion of jumbled voices made the speaker vibrate.

Egyptians and Israelis were talking together.

Three hours later, when the set had gone silent again, Slimane sighed. "At last! They've come to an agreement."

"Yes, they've come to an agreement," Simmy repeated thoughtfully.

But all the excitement and joy had gone out of them. During the course of their conversation over the radio they had learned the results of the conflict between the two nations.

It was true that the actual fighting had ceased. But the Israelis were occupying a portion of Egyptian territory, and skirmishes were frequent near the line of demarcation (the banks of the Suez Canal) where the two opposing forces had settled.

That the bitterness and antagonism still ran strong on both sides was very obvious from the tone of the exchanges between the Israelis and the Egyptians over the air.

The talks seemed to drag on forever. The two sides argued tensely about which country would be the first to come and pick up its own citizen. The men sounded frantic, almost insane, as they shouted back and forth.

The young people wondered why such a passionate argument should take place over so trivial a matter of procedure. What a horrible game of prestige! And for what?

The dispute over which country would take precedence over the other appeared all the more absurd since Simmy and Slimane had just proved that the hatred and bitterness were meaningless.

Simmy, worn out and furious at the endless arguments, was ready to cut them short when the two sides at last agreed that they would each send out a helicopter the following day. Both helicopters would touch down at exactly the same time, very near the two survivors. Even the number of passengers that each was to carry (five, including a doctor) was a matter to be negotiated.

When the final details were settled, Simmy turned to Slimane.

"They were certainly being terribly petty," she said.

"When it's a matter of destroying," Slimane said wryly, "soldiers are very efficient. They feel perfectly at home planning attacks and raids. But today they're faced with a new kind of problem, and they don't know how to deal with it. They just aren't used to helping people."

Simmy and Slimane did not go to bed

that night. They stayed awake, crouched in front of the fire, and together worked out their own plan for dealing with their rescuers.

✿   ✿   ✿

The helicopters touched down at precisely the same moment, each about fifty yards away, but on opposite sides of the place where Simmy and Slimane stood.

The passengers jumped down from the cabs and ran quickly out of range of the dangerous rotors. The blades continued to turn slowly for a few moments.

The men huddled together in two separate groups. No one could make up his mind to take in the first step. Then one of men in the Egyptian grouped called: "Slimane!"

Slimane recognized an officer from the company he had traveled with on the campaign, but he remained silent and didn't move.

The officer called again: "Slimane!"

Slimane stayed where he was, motionless, without saying a word.

From the opposite side an Israeli officer called: "Simmy!"

She made no move, standing silently as Slimane had done, watching the newcomers without showing the slightest trace of feeling.

The men in the two groups turned to each other and began to talk animatedly, almost angrily.

They seemed to be asking each other questions.

"It's certainly taking them a long while to make up their minds," Slimane whispered to Simmy.

Simmy's eyes were flashing, and she had a strange, new expression on her face. She said quietly:

"Well, I'm going to get them to make up their minds right now." Raising her voice, she called, "Well, did you come here to stare or to help?"

The men stared, puzzled and disturbed, but none made a move.

"So, your hatred is incurable," Simmy continued. "Are you afraid that if you meet you'll start fighting again? Can't you see how ridiculous it is? What are you waiting for?"

Simultaneously, the Egyptians and the Israelis sprang forward and rushed toward the girl and the boy.

"Shake hands," Simmy ordered.

The men watched Simmy, stupefied, and then turned and looked warily at each other.

"I said, shake hands," she repeated.

They had heard it correctly the first time; it was an order.

"I don't think any of you has leprosy," she continued, "but you're all infected with another disease: hatred. Come on, do what I say."

They obeyed her as if in a trance, holding out their hands tentatively. Then, looking at each other almost sheepishly, each took the hand of his opposite number. After that, the strain and tension between the

Egyptians and the Israelis began to relax visibly. But, when it came time to separate the boy and the girl, the uneasiness returned. It was then that Simmy insisted that they listen to what she had to say.

She had foreseen everything.

Though the men listened in silence, both sides, when Simmy had finished speaking, burst into a babble of objections. But neither Simmy nor Slimane would give in. At last the two headquarters were informed of the young people's demands. They argued and threatened, but Simmy was adamant. Finally, headquarters on both sides capitulated, and it was agreed that Slimane would go with Simmy and stay in Israel for three months. After that, Simmy would go to Egypt with Slimane and stay there for the same length of time. And then? Well, they'd see about that when the time came.

❖ ❖ ❖

Night had fallen.

They all ate together and then gathered

155

round the fire, mixing more comfortably now. They listened as Slimane and Simmy told of their experiences in the desert, and how they had managed to survive. They moved restlessly as Slimane and Simmy passionately described their dream of seeing friendship established among all the different peoples of the earth, each interrupting the other in their eagerness.

Passionate and determined though they were, the young people had no illusions about the extent of their own power or about the difficulties to be overcome. They were well aware that they might not live to see their dreams fulfilled. Still, while they lived, they would let nothing stop them. They would struggle against hatred and war until the day they died.

❊　❊　❊

It was time.
The helicopter blades began to turn.

Both sides waited as Simmy and Slimane said a final good-bye to the Sinai.

Even the most hardened of the men had been affected by the events of the previous night and by the friendship between the two young persons who had, only a short time before, tried to destroy each other. The men knew they would probably fight again, but some of their conviction would be gone, some of their blind hatred would have disappeared. And perhaps, some day, peace would come.